OH MY GODS! II
THE FORGOTTEN MAZE

Written by Stephanie Cooke & Insha Fitzpatrick
Art by Juliana Moon

WITHDRAWN

Etch
Clarion Books
Imprints of HarperCollinsPublishers

To Lily, Andy, Maria, and Whitney.
This book wouldn't be the same without you.

Etch and Clarion Books are imprints of HarperCollins Publishers.

Oh My Gods! 2: The Forgotten Maze
Text copyright © 2022 by Stephanie Cooke and Insha Fitzpatrick
Illustrations copyright © 2022 by Juliana Moon

Library of Congress Cataloging-in-Publication Data has been applied for.
ISBN: 978-0-358-29953-0 hardcover
ISBN: 978-0-358-29954-7 paperback

The text was set in Amescote.
Color by Whitney Cogar
Lettering by Andrea Miller
Edited by Lily Kessinger
Proofread by Susan Buckheit and Erika West
Cover and interior design by Andrea Miller

Manufactured in Spain
EST 10 9 8 7 6 5 4 3 2 1
4500840289

First Edition

THE CAFETERIA

LUNCHTIME

I have been promoted to editor in chief of *The Chariot*.

What's *The Chariot*?

What's *The Chariot*, Karen?!

It's only our school newspaper!

I didn't even know we *had* a school newspaper . . .

Well, that's going to change. *Everyone* is going to know we have a school paper soon.

Fresh content and new voices will turn it *all around!*

And who will these new voices be?

You all, of course!

What about me?

Putting you in charge of the weather seemed *boring*, so I was trying to think of the *perfect* thing for you.

And?

And . . . that's still up in the air.

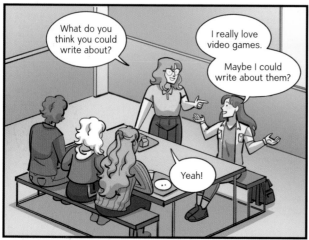

What do you think you could write about?

I really love video games.

Maybe I could write about them?

Yeah!

I've been meaning to show you, Dita, Pol, and Artemis my favorite game. This is the *perfect* excuse!

That's good, 'cause I already had the announcement printed up . . .

I'm on board!

The Chariot

THE CHARIOT PROMISES TO DELIVER FRESH CONTENT WITH NEW VOICES

MEET THE NEW TEAM**:

ATHENA—
Editor In Chief

HERMES—
Entertainment Editor

ARTEMIS—
Sports Editor

APOLLO—
Music Reviewer

APHRODITE—
Love Columnist

KAREN OF NEW JERSEY—
Columnist

THE FATES— *Horoscopes*

MEDUSA—
Editorial Assistant & Designer

**STAFF PHOTOGRAPHER WANTED—*APPLY NOW!*

LATER THAT EVENING . . .

HEY!!!!

C'mon! Follow me.

I thought she said there'd be pizza . . .

Shhhh!

Snickerdoodle!

Hey, Dad.

The pizza will be here soon! You don't want it to get cold.

The pizza will *survive*. I have something important to show my friends.

More important than *pizza?!*

See, *he* gets it!

There will be pizza!

Okay. Everyone gather around my computer.

Prepare to have your minds *blown!*

8

On a distant, remote planet . . .

. . . the fight for our galaxy is taking place.

Humans have taken the battle directly to the home planet of a fierce invading species known as the Høløs.

A small, elite military squadron from Earth is sent to the Hølø base to eliminate enemy leadership in what is surely a suicide mission.

But if they don't succeed, it could mean the end of the human race.

It's all up to . . .

MAJOR
HERNANDEZ

CAPTAIN
LISBETH
WELSH

CAPTAIN
HACKLER

FIRST
LIEUTENANT
IVAD

FIRST
LIEUTENANT
HOLLI
AITCH

SECOND
LIEUTENANT
AYALA WEST

Together, they are humanity's last hope.

HØLØHÜNTÉR

And *that's* the HØLØHÜNTÉR trailer!

This is the game you're always playing?

Yeah! It's honestly *the* best.

You can play a campaign solo, or you can play multiplayer modes like Capture the Flag, Deathmatch, Escort, Elimination, Survival.

And you can unlock secret modes and player maps through riddles and puzzles that players encounter!

I'm going to show you some of the sweet gameplay.

I only get to play with my friends back home once or twice a week.

They have a day off from school today, so they're gonna help me with this demo.

babaoop: Are your other friends there?!

Snipe_4_Lyfe: Do they think the game's dope?!

RekItRaj: How could they not?

Yes, they're here! And shush, they can *hear you!*

babaoop: Yeah, *and?!*

babaoop: Are you *embarrassed* of us?!

What? No, never!

Snipe_4_Lyfe: Quit messing around, then.

Let's just play the game already!

Y'all need some chill.

. . . you just have to survive for as long as you can.

BOOOOO!

Come *on!* That was baloney!

Why can't that player reload their bow faster?!

It's a *plasma* bow.

It's new to the game. It has a two-minute charging time.

If you just aim for their leader, it would take out the whole—

And *that's* how it's done.

Soooooooooo?

What'cha think?

I think it looks cool.

I want to pick a cute gamertag!

I want to try out some of my strategic theories within the game.

That was *awesome*. How do I get the plasma bow from the game?

That bow is definitely not real, Artemis.

So what do you think?

I can write about the game for the paper and introduce the school to the gaming world.

Hmmm . . . It's a fascinating game, but what's the angle?

I'm . . . I'm not sure . . .

Think about it a bit! You'll find your pitch for the article soon!

motherchaos: Kare, are you coming? We're starting a ranked match!

Coming! I'll be there after dinner.

I promised I'd play a ranked match. We're playing Capture the Flag.

You're welcome to hang out more and watch!

We'll start right after we have that pizza I promised.

YES, PIZZA! FINALLY.

We have to go after that though. Pol said he'd train with me.

I did not!

I have to head out after too. My moms want me to study for any surprise tests at school.

Yeah, I have to update my LoveJournal tonight.

Knock, knock! Did someone say *pizza?!*

Zed, you are the *best!*

Pfft, it was nothing.

And please, call me *Mayor.*

I'll see you at school!

POST-PIZZA

Message you later.

babaoop: About time.

I'm *back*, y'all!

RekItRaj: I'm launching the match now.

I *know* it's late, sorry! I was showing my friends the game.

Snipe_4_Lyfe: LET'S DO THIS!

RAJ: We did a good job! We'll be even better tomorrow!
AVERY: OH YEAH!
RAJ: U KNOW IT!
RACHAEL: PRY THIS GAME FROM MY COLD DEAD HANDS!
KAREN: Would y'all be cool if I invited my friends from here to play with us sometime?
RAJ: Of course!
JAELLE: We'll be normal, promise.
KAREN: Do you even know how to be normal?!
RACHAEL: WE'LL SEE, BAYBEEEE.

LATER . . .

HELLOOOOOOO, KARE BEAR!

Hey, Dad!

Dinner for tomorrow is in the oven!

Thanks!

It's casserole! Your mother gave me the recipe.

It smells great.

She says I can't let you have pizza *every* night . . .

Spoilsport . . .

Is everything okay, schnookums?

Yeah . . . I guess.

Hmmm, that doesn't sound okay to *me*.

It's silly . . .

If it has you upset, I bet it's not.

Thanks, Dad.

Our game was just interrupted.

I'm bummed that I didn't get to play with my friends more.

And you don't get to play with your friends again for a while?

Well, no . . .

We're playing again tomorrow, but this just makes it harder to be away from my friends back home.

That's understandable, sweetums.

You and your friends will always find time for each other though.

The good times will outweigh the bad in the end.

Thanks, Dad. Really.

I think I'm going to go to my room and hit the hay.

Okay, love bug. Sweet dreams!

22

Hey! I'm sorry I'm late.

motherchaos: No problem.

babaoop: Yeah, Avery's going full banshee like normal.

Snipe_4_Lyfe: EAT DIRT, RACHAEL.

RekItRaj: When are your friends gonna play with us?

Soon, hopefully! Tina just signed us up for the school newspaper, so it might be a while.

motherchaos: What's *your* job?

Games columnist. I want to write about *HØLØHÜNTÉR*, but I need to find the right angle.

babaoop: Ooh la la. Karen's gonna get too big for us, y'all.

Oh, shush!

I could never leave you.

RekItRaj: You ready to take down some Høløs in Survival Mode?

Snipe_4_Lyfe: I was *born* ready.

babaoop: OH, FANTASTIC.

BATTLEGROUND CHALLENGE: UNLOCK SECRETS

00:01:00

It might not be so bad!

If we get it right, the loot is sooooooo good!

babaoop: Yeah, but the last time, we got a battleground question *wrong*. We bombed so badly, we got mauled by four Hølø Berserkers.

Snipe_4_Lyfe: Maybe *someone* should stop shouting out answers.

Avery . . . I swear.

BATTLEGROUND CHALLENGE BEGINS
QUESTION: BEFORE THE HØLØ WAR, THE HØLØS DISGUISED THEMSELVES AS ANOTHER RACE TO EXPAND AND TAKE OVER THEIR PLANETARY ALIGNMENT. WHO WERE THEY?

I know this . . . I know this!

motherchaos: What's the answer?

Give me a minute!

We only *have* a minute!

00:00:30

Hello there.

Snipe_4_Lyfe: YOU AGAIN?!

babaoop: We need to report this player . . .

Kar3nat0r: I thought he'd go away after last time.

motherchaos: I'm trying to block him but it's not working.

REPORT A PLAYER
USERNAME: M1N0T4UR
ERROR—
COMMAND CANNOT BE
COMPLETED.
USER DOES NOT EXIST.

What the . . .

KAREN: M1N0T4UR just messaged me . . .

JAELLE: What did he say? Did you report it?!

KAREN: I did. He said, "Too bad you couldn't answer the question. Better luck next time."

RACHAEL: CREEPYYY.

RAJ: There has to be something we can do.

JAELLE: I'm gonna report him too and see about making the chat more private.

KAREN: It says his gamertag doesn't exist, so it's impossible to report him.

AVERY: UGH. This is so annoying.

RACHAEL: Whatever happened to our gaming happiness?

JAELLE: It's gonna be okay. We'll think of something.

RACHEL: OH YEAH.

AVERY: COME AND GET US, MINOJERK.

KAREN: *INSERT WARRIOR NOISE HERE*

THE FOLLOWING DAY . . .

WHOOOOOOSH!

Oh, good, you're here!

Yep. I sure am.

Walk with me.

Okay.

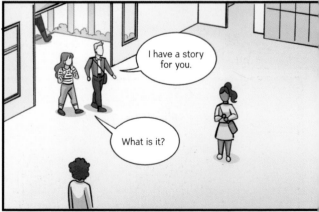

I have a story for you.

What is it?

You should head to the theater.

The theater?

Yeah. Talk to Ares. His stepbro has been missing for a couple of days.

Why give me this story?

Don't *you* want to cover it?

This story isn't really my style.

And you think it's *mine?!*

Well . . . you don't have a specialization like the rest of us.

So, I thought I'd throw you something juicy.

The Fates were pretty adamant that it had to be *you*.

They just had me deliver the message.

Make up a story.

Say you're covering auditions. Actors love a good headline.

Okay, fine.

Good! Head over ASAP.

That was good, Calypso.

We'll let you know what we decide.

Uh, hi there?

You'll find your assigned audition time slot on the schedule outside . . .

Oh, no no no no no!

I'm not an actor.

If you are not a thriving thespian, WHY are you in my theater?

I'm looking for Ares.

Backstage.

Oh, thanks!

33

Excuse me, I'm looking for Ares?

Ares?

Who's asking?

SIGH

35

Did you talk to Ares?

I did.

Are you going to do a story about his brother?

I don't know *how* to investigate a missing persons case!

But I *do* want to help him.

You gotta admit that it'll be a *great* story if you do figure it out.

What was that all about?

Hermes asked me to talk to Ares about his missing stepbrother.

Ah. And?

I think he wanted me to turn it into something I'm not comfortable with.

You know how he is. The more sensational and dramatic, the better.

Yeah—I do want to find a way to help Ares and Jeff.

More on that in a bit.

I think I know what my angle is!

You know that *HØLØHÜNTĒR* game I showed you?

Yeah!

41

I—I don't really know where to start.

Start with the facts. What do you know?

Write it all down and see where it takes you.

Yeah, okay. That makes sense.

I'll see what comes up.

I should get going.

Do you want to come to Ambrosia later?

We're going to talk about the last position we need for *The Chariot*.

Staff photographer!

I'd love to, but I think I'm going to do some research.

Okay!

We're playing Elimination Mode tonight, right?

RekItRaj: You got it!

babaoop: What's the game plan?

RekItRaj: We stay in formation and take out the Hσlσs.

If he turns up, we'll show him!

motherchaos: Not *that* plan. The plan for that M1N0T4UR guy if he makes an appearance.

Snipe_4_Lyfe: We play like normal. He might not even crash our game.

Snipe_4_Lyfe: Game faces, everyone!

SLAM!

I think the gamer troll is from Mt. Olympus.

What makes you think that?

How would he play the game *here*?

You've seen how behind our technology is.

It's just a hunch—

He said something that I've only *ever* heard here.

He said "oh my gods." With an "s."

I know it's not a lot to go on, but it's a start.

It *is* a stretch. You'll need more to support your theory.

I'm impressed, Karen. You're really showing a lot of initiative with *The Chariot*.

Thanks! I'm trying.

Anyways, I know it's not a big lead.

I'm hoping to find someone who can track down his account and see if they can tell where he's based.

You should talk to Arachne. She might be able to help.

Where can I find her?

She's usually in the theater at this time of year to help with the play. Check there first.

People really love the theater here.

Yeah. We're *super* dramatic.

How are *you?!*

How's the lighthouse coming along?

Things are great! The lighthouse is in better shape than ever.

And your sisters?

Eury and Stheno are great too. They seem happy. Eury even went into *town* the other day for the first time in years!

Whoa!

I know, right?!

Were you headed to the newspaper office? I hear you're helping out too!

Yeah! I was going to check in with Tina and see what I could do.

I went by earlier, but the Higher Authorities were talking to her.

I thought someone else was turned to stone, but they were looking for Jeff.

Jeff? Hopefully they found some leads.

I should let you get on your way, then.

It was *so* good to see you.

You should come over for dinner sometime!

I would *love* that!

Ares!

Hey!

55

Arachne! You still up here?

It is!

Ares, is that you?

You *never* come to visit me up here! What's the occasion?!

This is my friend Karen.

The new girl! Of course, hello.

Karen, this is Arachne.

I'm sure you've heard that we don't get a lot of new students here.

So, forgive me for already knowing a little bit about you.

Oh, uh, yeah. I've definitely noticed.

To what do I owe the pleasure?

I could *really* use your help.

What do you need?

Tina told me that you might be able to access some stuff on the web that we can't. Let me fill you in.

Let's go!

Interesting . . . Looks like he's had lots of different accounts before settling onto M1N0T4UR.

OOOOhooohhoohh!

OH, HO. WHAT'S THIS?!

This . . . this is very weird . . .

Did you find something?

What? What's wrong?

Well, to be fair, no one talks about it much these days.

There *used* to be this survivalist course in the basement.

It was meant to train students on track for the Hero Academy.

Hero Academy?

As they modernized the school, and the outside world changed, there wasn't really a need for it anymore.

So the course was shut down, and people stopped going down to the basement except to put stuff into storage.

But a *course*? In the *basement*?!

The new school was built over top of it, but it's still there.

No one should be going down there.

Sometimes a teacher sends a student down to place an item in storage. It's usually a punishment meant to scare them . . .

And M1N0T4UR might be down there somewhere?!

I should update Tina.

I'll come too.

Thank you *so* much for your help.

You rule, Arachne!

I'm happy to help! I hope you find what you're looking for.

If you need anything else, come find me.

You know how to make a gal blush, Ares.

Hey, Tina!

Hey, Karen! And hey, Ares! What are you doing here?

Oh! Ares might be our new staff photographer . . .

Really? We've been hoping to fill the position!

Uhhh . . .

No worries if you're still thinking about it.

I was right, Tina!

I wonder why M1N0T4UR is down there . . .

The old Hero Academy course *would* make a good defense if you wanted to hide, but why go to all that trouble?

Maybe he's planning something bigger?

That doesn't seem like this guy's MO.

He's been hiding behind anonymity in the *HØLØHÜNTĒR* game.

Yeah! But . . . it's like he's leaving bread crumbs?

What do you mean?

You got a new phone!

Yeah! It just arrived.

I looked up new models on Amazonia and found a deal!

I started looking right after you showed me yours.

I want your help in modernizing Mt. Olympus technology . . .

The new computer lab was the first step!

But we can talk about *that* later.

There!

Message sent. Hopefully the gang will be here soon.

A LITTLE WHILE LATER . . .

We're here!

Perfect timing.

Karen is investigating a story in the basement of the school.

We're heading down there soon, but we wanted to know if you'd come with us.

It *might* be dangerous . . .

I'm *in*.

Do you ever *not* carry that with you?!

Um, no? Who knows when I might need it, Karen.

Of course we'll come with you.

I—I really don't know what to expect down there.

What's your point?

I think what Artemis is *trying* to say is that it doesn't matter.

We're *not* going to let you go down there on your own.

You can head back to the theater. I know you have set pieces to work on.

Right, well . . .

Those pieces don't need to be put up until Hecate paints.

But I'd like to come along. Pretty sure the Higher Authorities haven't looked for Jeff there yet. And . . .

. . . I don't want to let you down for my first assignment as staff photographer.

Tina!

What?!
It's *POLICY!*

It's okay, Karen.

I'll sign the form.

You're officially a photographer with *The Chariot!*

Welcome aboard!

Uh, sorry, but what's *The Chariot*?

It's the name of the school paper! *Our* newspaper.

WHY DOES NO ONE KNOW THIS?!

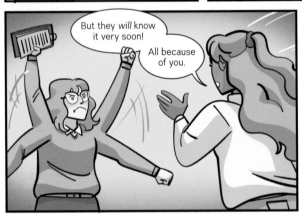

But they *will* know it very soon! All because of you.

Can we head out now?

Let's wait and start fresh tomorrow so we don't make our parents suspicious. It's almost dinnertime.

SIGH

Typical.

What *is* all this . . .

A basement in a basement . . .

I don't like the look of this.

Is that . . . a *maze?*

I think *that's* the training course I was talking about.

What is *that?!*

Or *who* . . .

M1N0T4UR . . .

Hey! Hey, you! We have a few questions . . .

Just a few?

WHO GOES THERE?!

Um, well, I'm Karen and—

ARE YOU PREPARED TO ENTER?

Uh . . . excuse me?

Enter what, exactly?

Yes, but what *is* the Minotaur's Maze?

It is . . .

. . . THE MINOTAUR'S MAZE!

Let's try this again . . .

What is the *purpose* of the maze?

It exists to test your resolve and resilience. To show the stuff that *true heroes* are made—

So, this is the training course.

It is . . .

. . . THE MINOTAUR'S MAZE!

WHOOOSH

THUNK

It—it's a robot . . .

So, this isn't the Minotaur that Karen is looking for?

It doesn't seem like it.

What?!

What are you all looking at?!

What do you want to do? Do you want to keep going?

This *is* your story.

What was that?

Just doing my job. Let's get going.

WHOOSH

Hmmm . . .

It's a riddle like the ones in *HØLØHÜNTÊR*.

In the game, the riddles unlock levels and secrets.

If we answer it correctly, maybe the door will open!

What happens if we get the answer wrong?

No need to worry about that 'cause I know the answer!

The answer is . . .

. . . PROMETHEUS!

Uh, Karen, are you *sure* that was the right answer?

Yes, I'm sure!

I think . . .

I *said*, the answer to the riddle is "PROMETHEUS."

Hmmm . . .

Earthquake?!

No, look! It's the door!

Time for
Phase Two . . .

Imagine students having to train in here . . .

Oh, I *am.*

It must've been *awesome!*

I really can't believe you sometimes, Art.

What?!

Whaa—

I'm glad you could make it.

I hope you like what I've done with the place.

Hmmm . . .

What is it, Karen?

This must be the next phase of the maze.

I think he's replicating Capture the Flag from *HØLØHÜNTÉR.*

It *all* comes back to *HØLØHÜNTÉR*.

The first time we encountered M1N0T4UR was after I showed you all the game.

Do you remember anything else about that match?

Hmmm . . .

We were playing Capture the Flag!

Maybe it's some twisted homage to you and your friends?

Maybe . . .

What do you think we can expect in this Capture the Flag game?

Give us a rundown.

Each team has a home base with a flag. They simultaneously need to protect their own flag while trying to steal the opposite team's flag from *their* home base.

The other team's flag needs to be brought back to your team's home base to win.

In *HØLØHÜNTÊR*, certain character classes are better suited for certain jobs.

So we should assign roles based on our strengths—like the newspaper!

Leave that to me!

Who's on the other team, then?

I'm gonna guess *they're* the other team.

Gods, I hope so!

Do they want us to *fight* the other team?

In *HØLØHÜNTÈR*, you would fight through anyone you came up against. In here . . . ?

Let's try to avoid that.

Party pooper . . .

Hmmm . . .

I'm not the goddess of strategy for nothing.

Based on what you've told me, here's who should be what . . .

Karen, you're playing Offense.

Supposing this *is* Capture the Flag, you need to get the enemy flag!

Artemis, you're playing Defense. We need your skills to protect *our* flag.

Dita! You'll be playing a dual role with Pol.

You'll be Defense and Support. Pol, you'll be Offense and Support. You guys need to protect and assist.

I'll be playing Support!

If anyone needs us to help or assist, yell "SUPPORT!"

And, Ares, we're going to need you to crush EVERYTHING!

I think we're ready.

Let's do this.

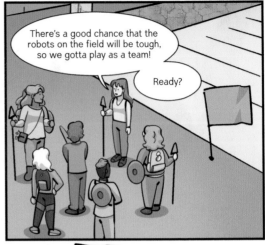

There's a good chance that the robots on the field will be tough, so we gotta play as a team!

Ready?

We've got this.

WELCOME TO PHASE TWO.

PHASE TWO
COMMENCING IN...

...3...

...2...

...1...

There's *no way* it's *that* easy . . .

Is this fog normally part of the game?

Huh?

No . . . weather mods are *very* unusual.

I *knew* it couldn't be this easy.

Quick, get the flag!

Pol and I will hold them off.

CLINK
CLINK

Come back here, you ugly robots!

It's okay, Karen. You can do this.

WHOOOSH

PHASE TWO, COMPLETE.

We did it!

Jeff?!

A-Ares?!

Good strategizing, Tina!

I know.

Real good job, team.

Real good.

Okay, but *why* are you here?

Well . . .

Before I knew it, I was lost. I came across the maze, and then entered after the big cow man told me to.

The Minotaur?

Yep, sure! Sounds about right!

And then I couldn't find my way out of *here* either!

That's *so* awful.

Yeah . . .

. . . I got in trouble and I was told to deliver some old files to the storage area.

I made it there and dropped off the box, but I got all turned around!

This long without pancakes has been *real* hard . . .

But then I saw you all enter the maze, and I decided to follow you.

I didn't realize Ares was with you until, well, now!

When we get back home, I'll make you all the pancakes you want.

REALLY?!

Promise.

Huh?

Pol! What's up?

Can we talk for a sec?

Sure, of course!

So, what did you want to talk about?

Uhhh . . .

Um, I just wanted to see if you're okay.

I've been noticing some stuff, and I, uh, just wanted to see how you're doing.

That's it?

Um, yeah.

Oh.

I'm fine.

I mean, I'm as *fine* as I can be in a weird training maze that's in the basement of our school.

You sure there wasn't something else you wanted to ask?

Uh, nope! Nothing else that I can think of.

Fine. Let's go back to the group, then.

Oh, okay.

Huh?

Everything okay, Kare?

Oh, uh . . .

Yeah.

Everything feels so surreal.

Even something normal like working on a story for the school newspaper has turned into . . .

. . . THIS!

This is *our* normal. Well . . . sort of.

I wanted to find a way to help make my gaming community better.

But I don't know what I'm doing.

It's really the only time I get to connect with my friends back home.

I miss them a lot.

I get why you're so passionate about this.

We'll get to the bottom of it.

What the—

What do we have to do here?

Well . . .

The second time M1N0T4UR crashed our game, it was in Survival Mode.

WHAT?!!?

Don't worry, Survival Mode isn't so bad!

It's usually just a few waves of Høløs.

But *Survival Mode?!* What happens if one of us gets killed while playing?

In the game, you just respawn!

There's usually a short amount of time out, and then you get brought back.

One of the robots respawned in the last match, remember?

Yeah, but he was a *robot*. What happens to *real people?!*

It'll be *fine!*

MOMENTS LATER . . .

And grab a short- *and* long-range weapon!

Remember that Survival Mode isn't as scary as it sounds!

Let's do this!

Here we go again.

PREPARE FOR PHASE THREE!

We need to hurry and get into position.

134

SECOND WAVE COMPLETE.

This next wave is the last . . .

Thank gods!

But it's also the hardest.

In the game, there're not just lots of Høløs. There are *different kinds.*

Massive ones, like the Hølø Generals and their Berserkers.

Berserkers?

FINAL WAVE!

Pol!

143

Kare?

I've been noticing you.

I mean, not like *that* . . .

Not that I wouldn't want to notice you like *that!*

What I mean is that I've been noticing these weird shifts in the weather.

When the sun gets blocked out, I tend to notice these things!

What does that have to do with me?

They happen around you. They happen when *you* have an emotional response.

A *strong* emotional response.

I noticed it when we first started looking for Medusa, but it's been getting more frequent.

Since we got here, there's been weird mist appearing.

Freak lightning storms.

Karen—*these* are your demigoddess powers.

Kare, are you okay?

I—I don't know what to say.

How am I supposed to control my powers? How am I supposed to live a *normal* life?!

You're living in Mt. Olympus. What's normal, anyways?

You'll figure it out.

The good news is that you don't have to figure it out on your own.

You have your dad. You have your friends. You have . . .

. . . me.

We should get back to the group.

Snacks! I ran out of mine this morning!

SWIPE

GRRRRRRRaa

Artemis!

SMACK

Jeff's been down here for *days!*

He needs that snack more than you do.

But I need to replenish my energy...

We should get moving.

Agreed.

I wanna get to the bottom of this before dinner!

Dinner?!

Did someone say *dinner?!*

Later, Jeff.

PREPARE FOR THE FINAL PHASE!

What do we do?!

Uhhh . . .

Well . . .

LOOK OUT!

RO

AAAR

What's the plan, Karen?

We're an easy target all together, so staying in smaller groups is our best option.

In smaller groups, it has to pick one group of us to focus on at a time.

Agreed.

Tina, you okay?

Yeah!

We should stay in separate groups.

To draw away its focus! Harder to pick a target if we *all* attack at once!

Pol and I will attack the monster head-on.

Artemis, you go with Ares and create a diversion. Try to draw away its attention.

Tina, go around to the other side of the monster.

Right!

What's the plan?!

To not get hit!

That's a good plan!

We divide and conquer each side—there's no way the Hydra can do anything but focus on one side or the other.

This is *not* good.

It's preparing to unleash its *ultimate* attack.

What does that mean?!

In the game, a hit from that attack would wipe everyone off the map. It would be game over.

What does it mean for *us*?

I—I don't know!

You *have* to use your powers.

I don't know *how* to use them!

We will figure out how to use them together, but you *have* to try.

If you don't try, who knows what will happen to us.

I haven't known you that long, but you are *so* strong, and so cool.

You moved to a new place, made all these new friends, and have already helped the community.

Not to mention all the tech you've introduced us to!

I admire you, Karen.

And I believe in you.

Everyone—

—get—

—back!

What *is* this
place?

M1N0T4UR . . .

M1N0T4UR!

M1N0T4UR!

Turn around *now!*

You're M1N0T4UR?

You're the one behind all of *this?!*

What's your name?

Your *real* name . . .

Minos.

Why did you do all of this?

Isn't it obvious?

How is any of *this* obvious?!

I did this for *you!*

I knew you'd appreciate what I created.

For *me?*

I reprogrammed all the old Hero Academy equipment so you could play *HØLØHÜNTER* for *real.*

You could've seriously hurt one of us!

But I didn't!

But you could've!

And you took away my time with my friends back home in the *actual* game.

I—

It is impossible to make friends here.

No one ever picked *me* in real life.

They make *fun* of me.

Minos, the *scrawny* Minotaur.

Who's ever even heard of a *scrawny* Minotaur?

My mom kept making me sign up for sports.

She said team activities would make me friends for life.

Then she gave up on that.

HA
HA
HA

We went on vacation to stay with a distant relative in New Jersey.

He had *HØLØHUNTER* at home.

It—it changed *everything*.

My cousin and I didn't get along well, but when we played the game, it was *almost* like we were friends.

It was . . .

It was nice.

Put that away.

Mooooooom!

I had to custom build a computer that could handle the game.

We're *hopelessly* behind on technology here.

Actually, I've been working on that with Karen!

Sorry!

At first, I was excited.

I thought I could play with my cousin and his friends— it's not like they could see the real me . . .

But even online, he didn't want to play with me.

HØLØHUNTER

NO FRIEND MATCHES AVAILABLE

Now that he didn't *have* to. He was embarrassed of me.

No one wanted to play with me.

So, I made my own fun.

What the—
What's happening to the game, man?!

My cousin found out that he really didn't like playing with me.

Man, I'm *out*. I don't have time for this . . .

He quit playing after a while, and I had no one to play with again . . .

As The Fates would have it, I came across you and looked at your profile.

I saw your IP coming from Mt. Olympus.

The only other player I've seen from here.

I watched you and your friends stream a game.

Even with the distance, you and your friends are so close . . .

I wanted that too.

So, you wanted to, what? Get our attention?

Yes, exactly!

I—

I thought if I could get your attention, you could see what I'd done.

I knew you'd appreciate it.

I'm sorry . . .

You could've *seriously* hurt one— or *all*—of us!

Jeff has been trapped down here for days!

I tried to let him out!

And when he didn't go through the exit, I left him food!

Jeff! Why didn't you just leave?!

You can't just *escape a maze* like that.

It was definitely a trap.

178

SIIIIIIGH.

It can be *really* hard to make friends.

But becoming a bully yourself is *not* an excuse.

I'm not a bully!

You crashed *our games* for attention.

Even if you didn't *mean* to be a bully, you still came across that way.

You don't make friends like that.

I'm not a soldier *for real.* None of us are.

Speak for yourself . . .

How did you even get all this stuff down here?

It took a while, but once I found the old freight elevator, it got a *lot* easier.

Elevator? Up to the school?

Yeah!

This *whole room* is an elevator.

After they built over the Hero Academy, they still wanted quick access to it, so they installed this!

So you built a computer room in here? And reprogrammed the old training tech?

Yeah . . .

Totally.

But maaaaaybe it's time to have a home base that's not so evil lair-y.

It'll take a while to disassemble everything and move it all.

Not if we all help.

Phew. That's all done at least.

How do we use the elevator?

Huh, how about that!

Thanks, but . . .

... I've got it from here.

We haven't finished moving the boxes yet.

I messaged my mom to help.

Are you sure? We can still help more.

No, it's okay.

My mom is here now.

Minos!

Thanks for coming, Mom.

What have you gotten yourself into now, Minos? What is all of this? Why are you at school on a weekend?

I found a maze in the school basement . . .

Okay, then.

I guess we'll see you around.

Minotaurs *do* love mazes!

Yeah.

See you around.

Hey, Minos!

If you ever want to play *HØLØHÜNTÊR* without doing . . . ALL OF THIS . . .

. . . let me know . . . I'm sure my friends wouldn't mind another player joining our lineup!

I'm *FREE!*

We survived the maze!

I could *really* use a nap.

I could really use some protein.

Or some ambrosia!

Mmmm, ambrosia . . .

WHOOMP!

MOOn_g0ddess51:
WE DID IT!

Snipe_4_Lyfe:
Kare, these new
friends of yours?

I APPROVE.

fr0m0lympusWluv:
Should we be worried
about that?

h00tdini525:
Naaaaah.

CONTINUED FROM COVER

Many readers of *The Chariot* will not know what *HØLØHŪNTĒR* is. It's a video game—a great video game—that I love dearly. The story is fun and makes me smile, but it's how it connects people—and, more specifically, my friends that I left behind in New Jersey—that makes it special to me. Recently, we had to deal with someone who took the fun away from the game for us. They trolled us until we stopped playing for a while. The gamer turned out to be a fellow student who walked amongst us. Initially, I set out to expose them and to bring attention to a larger issue that plagues gamers, but I don't want to keep the cycle of toxicity going.

Instead, I'd like to talk to you about learning to be yourself and embracing who you are. Since coming to Mt. Olympus, I've learned that my dad is a god and I myself am a demigoddess! It's crazy, right? Except it's not! And now on top of all of that, I have to learn how to control a new set of powers and figure out even more about myself, all while trying to figure out everything else.

I know this probably doesn't seem like a real big problem to a lot of people. This time last year, if someone had told me that having powers was any kind of a possibility, I would have laughed. Everyone back home wants super-powers—who doesn't want to be a hero like they see in comic books? Having power is a whole lot of responsibility, and that is my reality now. I don't just have a personal obligation to figure out my powers, but I have a moral responsibility to understand them—and to hopefully never use them to hurt anyone, whether that's accidental or on purpose.

I want to use my powers and my experiences in the world so far to help shape things for the better. And I'm lucky to have great friends to help me hone my gifts and share moments with. While many at Mt. Olympus do *actually* have honest-to-gods powers, the *true* power here, for me, is friendship.

Hey!

What's *that* you're reading?

You *know* what it is, Tina.

Well, *soooooorry* for being excited!

C'mon, Artemis! Let Tina have this moment.

She worked *so* hard to make it happen!

Thank you, Karen. At least someone appreciates what I've done. What we've *all* done.

Honestly, Tina. It turned out *really* good.

Yeah, Tina! It's incredible.

Ahh, thank you.

You should be so proud!

I couldn't have done it without all of you.

So, thank you.

CONTENTS

CODING CLUB

Join today and learn about the tech of the future!
Talk to Arachne or Minos to join.

COMING SOON:
Mt. Olympus's Biggest Battle of the Bands

Featuring a special performance from last year's winners and
touring sensation, THE HARPIES!
Lead singer Celaeno of THE HARPIES will serve as a guest judge for the battle
and help us decide who is the best of the best!

SIGN UP NOW!

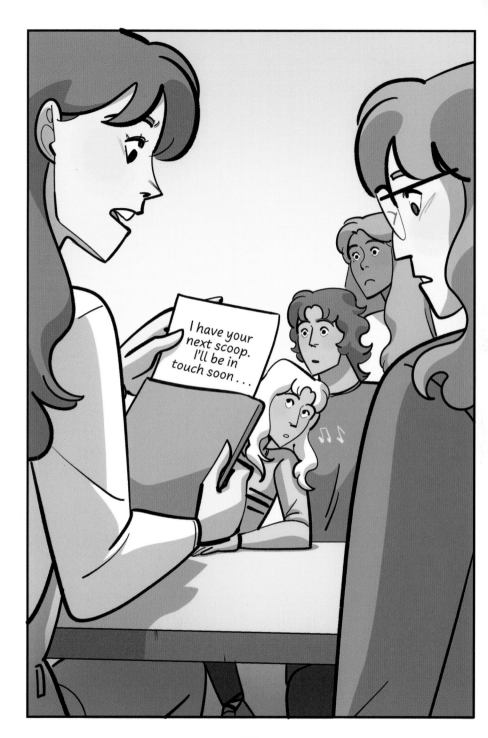

KAREN'S MYTHOLOGY NOTES!!!

Ares seems all tough on
the outside, but he's
actually a big softy?
He REALLY cares about
Jeff and making sure
he's safe. I get a good
vibe from him... ♡

ARES

Ares is the god of war. This god has a love of
violence and the battlefield. Ares is the oldest son
of Zeus and Hera, and has two sisters, Hebe, the
goddess of youth, and Eileithyia, the goddess of
childbirth. Ares is known for fighting and having
a bad temper. Even though many gods disliked
him, he was loved by women. He fell in love with
Aphrodite while she was married to her husband,
Hephaestus. Ares is known for his war gear,
including his helmet, spear, and Greek armor. He
has been known to battle many different gods
and demigods. Hercules was one of those gods.
Hercules managed to hurt Ares in a fight even
though Athena, the goddess of war, protected him.

At first, I was like, ?
is that a spider girl? ?
But then I was all like,
\\\|//\\\\|//\\\\|//
GO SPIDER GIRL!!!
//|\\\ //|\\\ //|\\\
She's just...so cool?

ARACHNE

Born in the village of Hypaepa, Arachne is
the daughter of a wool dyer. Arachne has an
incredible ability for spinning and weaving. She
was known throughout her town for it and
boasted frequently about her skills without giving
credit to Athena, also the goddess of handicrafts
and the arts. In retaliation, Athena decided to
disguise herself as an old woman and challenge
the girl to a spinning and weaving competition.
Once Arachne accepted, Athena unveiled herself
to be a goddess. Despite this, Arachne still made
the finest tapestry anyone—mortal or god—had
ever seen. Athena was so angry at the girl that
she hit her over the head, which led to her death.
However, something happened afterwards—
Arachne turned into a spider! Now she can use
her skill as she pleases for all time.

MINOS (THE MINOTAUR)

Asterion, more commonly known as the Minotaur, is a half-man, half-bull creature born of Queen Pasiphae and a white bull. King Minos, Pasiphae's husband, was told by the god Poseidon to kill the bull because Poseidon believed he could make anyone do anything for him. However, King Minos couldn't bring himself to harm it. As punishment, Poseidon cursed Pasiphae to fall in love with the bull. When the Minotaur was born, King Minos locked him away in a labyrinth on the advice of an oracle from Delphi, a sanctuary built to honor the god Apollo. The maze structure was built in Knossos and designed by Daedalus, a craftsman. After King Minos's son was killed in battle by Athenians, Athens sent fourteen youths to the Minotaur every nine years as a sacrifice, as the youths couldn't escape the labyrinth and were devoured. Theseus, a young hero from Athens, volunteered and successfully went through the labyrinth with the help of Ariadne, King Minos's daughter. When he found the Minotaur, they engaged in a heavy battle before the Minotaur was ultimately destroyed.

Wow, that sounds terriBULL... Minos had a LOT going on in his life...past life? I'm glad he doesn't eat people anymore. 😋

> Baby steps! <

JEFF

Jeff is a happy-go-lucky student at Mt. Olympus Junior High. He's not in any history books (yet), but he doesn't let that ever get to him. He knows his worth and he strives to be kind and friendly to everyone around him. Besides, who needs a lasting legacy when you have *pancakes?!* Jeff's stepsibling is Ares, and they have a special brotherly bond. Jeff has no powers . . . that he knows of. Unless the Power of Pancakes counts (and he would say that it does).

I like snacks as much as the next person, but Jeff REALLY likes them. And pancakes? Don't get him started! Can you be addicted to pancakes?

BIBLIOGRAPHY

- Giesecke, Annette. *Classical Mythology A to Z: An Encyclopedia of Gods & Goddesses, Heroes & Heroines, Nymphs, Spirits, Monsters, and Places.* New York: Black Dog & Leventhal, 2020.
- Hamilton, Edith. *Mythology: Timeless Tales of Gods and Heroes.* New York: Black Dog & Leventhal, 2011.
- Kershaw, Stephen, and Victoria Topping. *Mythologica*. Minneapolis: Wide Eyed Editions, 2019.

QUIZ: WHICH CHARACTER FROM *HØLØHŪNTĒR* ARE YOU?

1) WHAT DO MOST PEOPLE CONSIDER YOUR BEST TRAIT?
A. Your protective nature
B. Your caring side
C. Your violent side
D. You can find anything in seconds
E. You get back up after being knocked down
F. Your kindness

2) QUICK! THE HØLØS ARE ATTACKING! WHAT'S YOUR FIRST ACTION?!
A. Pick up a weapon and lead the charge
B. Help the captain as their backup
C. BLAST THEIR ROBO BUTTS BACK TO WHEREVER THEY CAME FROM
D. Find out where these Høløs are coming from
E. Get a blaster and start firing away
F. Try not to hurt anyone TOO badly

3) WHAT DO YOU WANT TO BE WHEN YOU GROW UP?
A. A leader
B. You don't remember
C. An artist
D. A musician
E. An athlete
F. A writer

4) WHAT'S YOUR FAVORITE LEVEL IN *HØLØHŪNTĒR?*
A. Capture the Flag
B. Deathmatch
C. ALL OF THEM
D. Elimination
E. Survival
F. Escort

5) THE HØLØS HAVE CAPTURED YOU. THERE'S NO WAY TO ESCAPE! WHAT DO YOU DO?

A. Come up with a course of action with your team
B. Figure out any riddles or puzzles the Høløs may have
C. INSULT THEM: "SILLY ROBO JERKS. LET US GO!!!"
D. Calculate how much time the team has until the Høløs fry you
E. Try to pick the locks of your chains
F. Get scared, maybe cry a bit (MAYBE)

6) YOU'RE A NATIONAL HERO FOR DEFEATING THE HØLØS! HOW DO YOU CELEBRATE?

A. Eat MASSIVE amounts of cake
B. Sit down with a good book
C. Go out on the town! THE NIGHT IS YOUNG!
D. Update your systems
E. Join the night out on the town
F. Call your parents and let them know you're okay!

RESULTS

Mostly As—You are MAJOR HERNANDEZ
You're a natural-born leader! Major Hernandez is the top-ranking officer in Squadron 1.002. You're a person who wants everyone you care about to be okay, but you won't stand for nonsense either! You're supportive but have strong boundaries.

Mostly Bs—You are CAPTAIN LISBETH WELSH
You're a caring person, but you aren't afraid to kick butt when you need to. Captain Lisbeth Welsh lost her memory, but found a place alongside her fellow Hunters. You're usually down for a quiet night rather than a loud one, and you know a good book when you read one.

Mostly Cs—You are CAPTAIN HACKLER
You are the LIFE of the party! Captain Hackler is bloodthirsty, carefree, and a criminal. However, that won't stop people from loving you. You're 100% the wildest person imaginable, and you are the funniest person in any room.

Mostly Ds—You are FIRST LIEUTENANT IVAD (INTER-VERSATILE ARTIFICIAL DROID)

You're the smartest person anyone knows! First Lieutenant IVAD is an artificial droid, yet has the biggest heart. You enjoy research and also music (of all genres). You're fiercely independent, but you love working as a team and sharing your knowledge with everyone.

Mostly Es—You are FIRST LIEUTENANT HOLLI AITCH

You're super chill and not afraid of hard work! Holli Aitch used to be the golden child of the Hunters, but after seeing her squadron get destroyed by Høløs, she struggled to continue as team leader, paralyzed by the fear of being responsible for her team's safety. You work hard to make sure everyone's okay. Don't forget to take time out for yourself.

Mostly Fs—You are SECOND LIEUTENANT AYALA WEST

You're the newbie! You're kind, ambitious, and happy to be learning all you can to figure out who YOU are. Ayala West has seen the destruction that Høløs have wreaked on her planet, and she wants revenge! However, you're still a little scared about fighting; but if someone hurts you (or your loved ones), you'll make them PAY!!!!